MARC BROWN

Arthur Flips!

Arthur's father woke up sick. "Achoo!" he sneezed. "I mean, good morning. I've got to get up and make the pancakes for our neighborhood breakfast."

"I don't think so," said Mom. "You've got a terrible cold."

"Who's going to cook the pancakes?" asked Dad.

"Whoever heard of a pancake breakfast without pancakes?" said D.W.

"What about us?" said Arthur. "We can make the pancakes. And I know who can help."

"This is a big job," said Dad.

"Don't worry, dear," said Mom. "We can do it."

Mom called Grandma Thora to help.

"I'll be the pancake taster," offered D.W

Arthur's friends wanted to help, too.

"Look at all this great stuff!" Buster cried. "I feel like a chef!"

"Cool!" said Binky.

"I could perform some interesting science experiments here," said the Brain.

"We can make my famous pineapple upside-down pancakes,"
said Francine. "The crowd will love them!"

Binky crushed a handful of potato chips with his fist.
"What about my amazing potato chip pancakes?"

"What is *that* supposed to be?" asked Muffy.

"Orion," the Brain explained. "I'm making my constellation cakes."

"They can't be as good as my silver dollar pancake kabobs," said Muffy. "I use rainbow sprinkles!"

"Mmm...tasty," said Buster. He added some ice cream to the goopy mixture.

"Let's make it *really* tasty," said Arthur, adding whipped cream and a cherry.

"We better get to work," Francine said. "We've got a lot to do."

"Here's what we'll need for my silver dollar kabobs," Muffy said.

"Who said we're making those?" asked Binky.

"I just want to make the best pancakes," said Muffy.

"Who says your pancakes are the best?" asked Francine.

"Yeah!" Buster added. "I think the Brain's are better."

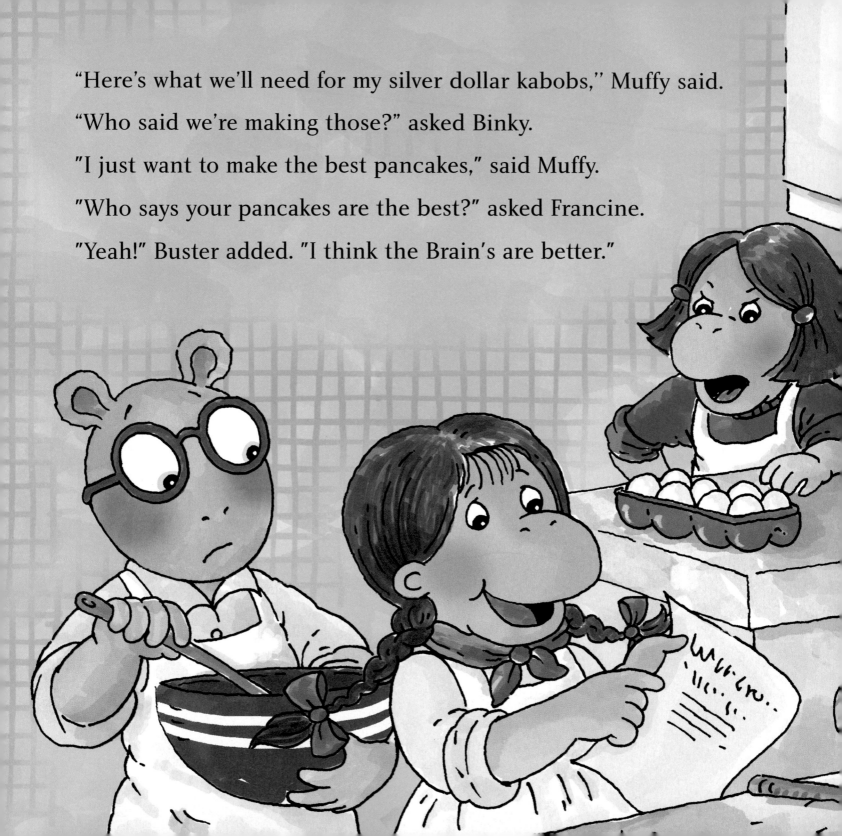

Everyone started to argue. "I think we should make pineapple...what about potato chips...the pancakes need sprinkles!"

Everyone was talking, but no one was listening.

"We have to decide whose pancakes we're going to make,"
Buster said. "The doors open any second."

"I have an idea!" said Arthur.
"We could each make our
own recipe."

"Arthur's right," Francine said.
"Let's write up a menu so
everyone can choose."

Arthur's pancake team went to work.

Grandma Thora took the orders. Arthur's mom mixed the batter and poured it into several bowls. Then Francine, Muffy, the Brain, and Buster each added their special ingredients.

"I'll pour," Binky said, "while Arthur flips!"

The orders started coming faster and faster. Arthur and his friends worked like crazy.

"Two constellation cakes, a silver dollar kabob, and a pineapple upside-down!" called Grandma Thora.

There were pancakes everywhere!

After breakfast Mrs. Sipple congratulated Arthur and his friends. "What a team!" she cried. "This has been our most successful pancake breakfast ever!"

"I'm tired," said Arthur.

"Me, too," Francine agreed.

"Me, three," said Muffy.

"Arthur, guess what?" said D.W. "I just volunteered all of us to cook the big spaghetti dinner at the firehouse next month."

"I make a great meatball sundae!" said Buster.